D1537424

characters created by

lauren child

I am EXTREMELY
absolutely boiling

Grosset & Dunlap

Charlie and Lola™

Text based on the script written by Bridget Hurst

Illustrations from the TV animation produced by Tiger Aspect

GROSSET & DUNLAP
Published by the Penguin Group
Penguin Group (USA) Inc., 375 Hudson Street, New York, New York 10014, USA
Penguin Group (Canada), 90 Eglinton Avenue East, Suite 700, Toronto, Ontario M4P 2Y3, Canada
(a division of Pearson Penguin Canada Inc.)
Penguin Books Ltd., 80 Strand, London WC2R 0RL, England
Penguin Group Ireland, 25 St. Stephen's Green, Dublin 2, Ireland
(a division of Penguin Books Ltd.)
Penguin Group (Australia), 250 Camberwell Road, Camberwell, Victoria 3124, Australia
(a division of Pearson Australia Group Pty. Ltd.)
Penguin Books India Pvt. Ltd., 11 Community Centre, Panchsheel Park, New Delhi—110 017, India
Penguin Group (NZ), 67 Apollo Drive, Rosedale, North Shore 0632, New Zealand
(a division of Pearson New Zealand Ltd.)
Penguin Books (South Africa) (Pty.) Ltd., 24 Sturdee Avenue,
Rosebank, Johannesburg 2196, South Africa

Penguin Books Ltd., Registered Offices: 80 Strand, London WC2R 0RL, England

Library of Congress Control Number: 2008040920

ISBN 978-0-448-45180-0   10 9 8 7 6 5 4 3 2 1

I have this little sister, Lola.
She is small and very funny.
"I am also extremely absolutely BOILING!
And the only thing that will make me completely
NOT boiling anymore is a strawberry ice cream!"

Outside in the shade,
I ask, "Arnold, why are
you **panting**?"

Arnold says,
"Dogs keep **cool** by **panting**.
I'm trying to see
if it works."

Lola says,
"Could you pant
more quieter please?"

Then I say,
"I hear the ice cream truck!"

Lola says,
 "Yum, strawberry!"

"Mmm . . . yummy,"
 says Arnold.

Then Lola says,
 "I know, Arnold!
I'll taste your ice cream
and then you can
   taste mine."

"Okay. Me first,"
 says Arnold.

Arnold takes a big lick
of Lola's ice cream,
   but when Lola
tries to take it back . . .

"Oh, no!" shouts Lola.
"My ice cream is COMPLETELY
all over the floor!"

"Maybe Arnold
will share his ice cream
with you," I say.

So Lola asks,
"Arnold, will you share your
ice cream with me?"

But Arnold says, "No."

And Lola says,
"You are not my
favorite or my best.
I will not ever
never forgive you!"

Later, Lola says,
"Ice is good
for **cooling**, but not
as nice-tasting
as ice cream."

"I wish we were in
the North Pole," I say.

"Yes," Lola says.
"Where it is completely
freezing cold."

Marv and Morten pass by
on their way to
the swimming pool.

Lola asks,
"Can we come, too?"

But Marv says,
"Sorry, Lola. There isn't any
room in the car.
Maybe you could
play with Arnold?"

"I'm not playing
with him," says Lola.
"He's a meanie!"

Instead of going
to the pool,
   Lola and I make
a waterfall.

"All the water's gone,"
   Lola says.

"That's okay," I say.
   "We'll get more
from the hose."

That's when we see
Arnold . . . and his pool.

So I say,
"That would DEFINITELY
cool us down.
Don't you think,
Lola?"

But Lola says,
"Come on, Charlie . . ."

"It might be a really,
        really good idea to
forgive Arnold," I say.
            "Then maybe you
can play in a real pool."

"But he didn't **share**
            OR say he's sorry,"
says Lola.

"Well, he looks sorry," I say.

"Does he?" Lola asks.

    Then Arnold calls out,
"Lola, would you like
            to sit in my pool?"

Lola finally says,
"Yes, please."

And Arnold says,
"I'm sorry about the
ice cream, Lola."

"That's okay," says Lola.
"Do you want to play
squirty bottles?"

"Yes, please," he says.

"Charlie!" Lola shouts.
"Can you pass Arnold
a squirty bottle?"

"I can't," I say. "Arnold's
dad gave us ice pops!"

"ICE POPS!" Lola says.

PLOP!
Arnold's ice pop falls
into the pool.

"My ice pop!" says Arnold.

So Lola asks,
"Do you want a bit of mine?"

And Arnold says,
"Thanks, Lola."

But then . . .

PLOP!
Lola's ice pop falls into the pool, too.
"Oops," Arnold says.
And Lola says, "Charlie . . . ?"

12/09